For A.A.

First published 1994 by Walker Books Ltd
87 Vauxhall Walk, London SE11 5HJ

This edition produced 1999 for
The Book People Ltd, Hall Wood Avenue
Haydock, St Helens WA11 9UL

© 1994 Tony Kenyon

Printed in Hong Kong

ISBN 0-7445-2668-X

Pat·A·Cake

Tony Kenyon

TED SMART

Pat-a-cake, pat-a-cake, baker's man,

bake me a cake
as fast as you can.

Pat it,

and prick it,

and mark it with b,

and put it
in the oven

for baby ...

and me!